MW00905316

A Little Something ...

FOR YOU!

* Sarah

A Little Something

by
Sarah Hartt-Snowbell

illustrated by
June Bradford

a Napple

Copyright ©1998 Sarah Hartt-Snowbell

All rights reserved. No part of this publication may be reproduced, stored
in a retrieval system or transmitted, in any form or by any means, electronic,
mechanical. photocopying, recording or otherwise, without the prior written
consent of the publisher.

Napoleon Publishing
An imprint of TransMedia Enterprises Inc.
Toronto Ontario Canada

Le Conseil des Arts
du Canada
DEPUIS 1957 | The Canada Council
for the Arts
SINCE 1957

We acknowledge the support of the Canada Council for the Arts for our publishing program.

Canadian Cataloguing in Publication Data

Hartt-Snowbell, Sarah, 1942-
   A little something

ISBN 0-929141-60-1

I. Bradford, June. II. Title

PS8565.A676L57 1998   jC813'.54   C98-931872-9
PZ7.H37Li 1998

I dedicate *A Little Something* to my mother, Cypra Richler-Hershcovich, who enriched my life with love, poetry and whimsical thoughts.

My heartiest thanks to Peter Carver and members of the George Brown College Writing-for-Children group for their extensive support and confidence.

On a windy Monday morning
on the seventeenth of May,
Sandy's Daddy slept too much
and roared, "I'm LATE today!"

He shaved his bristly whiskers,
combed his teeth and brushed his hair,
and gobbled down his eggs and toast—
he had no time to spare.

As Daddy hurried through the gate,
SOMETHING went amiss,
and then, a most peculiar thing
happened... just like this...

A Little Something
tumbled
through the big front
door.
It did a twirly
somersault
and
landed
on
the floor.

No one heard a crash
or a splat
or ker-plunk
or a rattle
or a clatter
or a clang
or a clunk.

The Little Something
skittered
to a corner
where it huddled,
looking
very shy
and timid
and baffled
and befuddled.

The cat saw it first
and chased it 'round the room,
then it scurried through the kitchen,
and hid behind the broom.
It perked up the puppy,
who chased it up the wall,
then it zigged across the ceiling,
and zagged along the hall.

Little Sandy saw it
and joined the lively chase,
and it wasn't very long until
Mom was in the race.

The Little Something sque-e-e-zed
through a crack in the door
and flew around the corner,
past the candlestick store.

They followed very briskly,
but they couldn't pin it down,
as they darted down the road
to the very next town.

They dashed along behind it
in the sunshine and the rain,
over cars and trucks and buses
and a big freight train.

They skipped along the rooftops
and cartwheeled over trees,
as the Little Something fluttered by...
riding on the breeze.

The wind scooped them up
and much to their surprise,
they were drifting on a cloud
in the bright blue skies,

flying over Fleegledown,
north of Jagged-Rock,
past the Banks of Bazzarazz,
Yabooki and Kappok.

They glided down a rainbow
way above the county zoo,
and tumbled
toward the pocket
of a mama kangaroo.

They wriggled and they jiggled
with every mighty jump,
then they spied
the Little Something
on a dromedary hump.

So they boarded the giraffe
'til they reached
sooOO high,
but the wind tipped them over
topsy-turvy in the sky.

They soared beyond the gates
above the chim...pan...zee,
and bounded down the highway
to the billows of the sea.

Mom and Little Sandy
and the puppy and the cat
surfed the rolling waves
on a baseball bat.

They saw the Little Something
riding high
upon a whale,
and swam along behind
to grab
its awesome slipp'ry tail . . .

But the whale took a dive
and swirled down below,
where it flipped and it flopped
'til they had to let go.
They waved to the salmon
and the lobster and, of course,
to the shark and the oyster
and the old seahorse.
The octopus waved,
eight times at the most,
as they all left the ocean
and scrambled to the coast.

They scampered up the hills
through the woods and by the bay,
and pursued the Little Something —
but...it always got away!

They'd tracked the Little Something
to the east and to the west,
down the deep, dark valleys,
and above the highest crest,

through the vast sandy desert,
and the squooshy, soggy bog,
in a sun-dazzled haze,
and in drizzle and in fog.

They followed north and south,
on the ground and in the air,
on a ragged-jagged journey
through the Land of Everywhere.

Little Sandy cried, "Look!
Now the sky is turning black,
and we're never gonna catch it...
Do we hafta turn back?"

The Little Something
seemed to fade,
and drifted out of sight —
so they turned
and hurried homeward
in the shadows of the night.

What's the Little Something?
Where did it start?
The Little Something sprang to life —
right from Daddy's heart.

For when Daddy left for work that day
he threw a little kiss —
he was all a hurry-scurry
and he didn't mean to miss.

But the kiss got lost
as it flew from Daddy's hand,
and it searched all day
for a perfect place to land.

The kiss whirled around
with a long a mighty leap,
as they'd finished eating dinner
and drifted off to sleep.

Then it wafted and it dipped
like a feather in the sky,
and floated through the window,
With a tiny, joyful sigh.

It glimmered in the darkness
though it felt a little weak,
and settled very softly...
on Little Sandy's cheek.